TRUCKSTOP
AND OTHER
LAKE WOBEGON
STORIES

GARRISON KEILLOR

TRUCKSTOP
AND OTHER
LAKE WOBEGON
STORIES

penguin books

PENGUIN BOOKS

Published by the Penguin Group

Penguin Books USA Inc., 375 Hudson Street,
New York, New York 10014, U.S.A.
Penguin Books Ltd, 27 Wrights Lane,
London W8 5TZ, England
Penguin Books Australia Ltd, Ringwood,
Victoria, Australia
Penguin Books Canada Ltd, 10 Alcorn Avenue,
Toronto, Ontario, Canada M4V 3B2
Penguin Books (N.Z.) Ltd, 182–190 Wairau Road,
Auckland 10, New Zealand

Penguin Books Ltd, Registered Offices:
Harmondsworth, Middlesex, England

Published in Penguin Books 1995

"January" is from the chapter entitled "Winter" in *Lake Wobegon Days*.
The other stories are from *Leaving Home*. Both books are published by
Penguin Books.

ISBN 0 14 60.0109 5

Printed in the United States of America

CONTENTS

Truckstop

It has been a quiet week in Lake Wobegon. Florian and Myrtle Krebsbach left for Minneapolis on Tuesday, a long haul for them. They're no spring chickens, and it was cold and raining, and he hates to drive anyway. His eyesight is poor and his '66 Chev only has 47,000 miles on her, just like new, and he's proud of it. But Myrtle had to go down for a checkup. She can't get one from Dr. DeHaven or the doctors in Saint Cloud because she's had checkups from them recently and they say she is all right. She is pretty sure she might have cancer. She reads "Questions and Answers on Cancer" in the paper and has seen symptoms there that sound familiar, so when she found a lump on the back of her head last week and noticed blood on her toothbrush, she called a clinic in Minneapolis, made an appointment, and off they went. He put on his good carcoat and a clean Pioneer Seed Corn cap, Myrtle wore a red dress so she would be safe in Minneapolis traffic. He got on Interstate 94 in Avon and headed south at forty miles an hour, hugging the right side, her clutching her purse, peering out of her thick glasses, semis blasting past them, both of them upset and scared, her about brain tumors, him about semis. Normally she narrates a car trip, reading billboards, pointing out interesting sights, but not now. When they got beyond the range of the "Rise 'N Shine" show, just as Bea and Bob were coming to the "Swap 'N Shop" feature, a show they've heard every morning for thirty years, they felt awful, and Florian said, "If it was up to me, I'd just as soon turn around and go home."

It was the wrong thing to say, with her in the mood she was in, and she was expecting him to say it and had worked up a speech in her mind in case he did. "Well, of course. I'm sure you would rather turn around. You don't care. You don't care one tiny bit, and you never have, so I'm not surprised that you don't now. You don't care if I live or die. You'd probably just as soon I died right now. That'd make you happy, wouldn't it? You'd just clap your hands if I did. Then you'd be free of me, wouldn't you— then you'd be free to go off and do your dirty business, wouldn't you."

Florian, with his '66 Chev with 47,003 miles on it, wouldn't strike most people as a candidate for playboyhood, but it made sense to her—forty-eight years of marriage and she had finally figured him out, the rascal. She wept. She blew her nose.

He said, "I would too care if you died."

She said, "Oh yeah, how much? You tell me."

Florian isn't good at theoretical questions. After a couple minutes she said, "Well, I guess that answers *my* question. The answer is, you don't care a bit."

It was his idea to stop at the truckstop, he thought coffee would calm him down, and they sat and drank a couple cups apiece, and then the pie looked good so they had some, banana cream and lemon meringue, and more coffee. They sat by the window, not a word between them, watching the rain fall on the gas pumps. They stood up and went and got in the car, then he decided to use the men's room. While he was gone, she went to the ladies' room. And while she was gone, he got in behind the wheel, started up, checked the side mirror, and headed out on the freeway. Who knows how this sort of thing happens, he just didn't notice, his mind was on other things, and Florian is a man who thinks slowly so he won't have to go back and think it over again. He was still thinking about how much he'd miss her if she was gone, how awful he'd feel, how empty the house would be with him lying alone in bed at night, and all those things when you want to turn to someone and say, "You won't believe what happened to me," Or "Did you read this story in the newspaper about the elk in Oregon?" or "Boy, Johnny Carson is looking old, ain't he? And Ed too," and she wouldn't be there for him to point this out to—and he tuned to tell her how much he'd miss her and she wasn't there. The seat was empty. You could have knocked him over with a stick.

He took his foot off the gas and coasted to a stop. He hadn't noticed her crawl into the backseat, but he looked and she wasn't there. She hadn't jumped—he would've noticed that. (Wouldn't he?) It couldn't've been angels taking her away. He thought of the truckstop. He was a good ways from there, he knew that. He must've gone twenty miles. Then, when he made a U-turn, he noticed he wasn't on the freeway anymore. There was no median strip. He was on a Highway 14, whatever that was.

He drove a few miles and came to a town named Bolivia. He never knew there was a Bolivia, Minnesota, but there it was. Went into a Pure Oil station, an old man was reading a Donald Duck comic book. Florian asked, "How far to the Interstate?" He didn't look up from his comic. A pickup came in, the bell dinged, the old man kept reading. Florian went down the street into a cafe, Yaklich's Cafe, and asked the woman where the Interstate was. She said, "Oh, that's nowheres around here." "Well, it must be," he said, "I was just on it. I just came from there."

"Oh," she says, "that's a good ten miles from here."

"Which way?"

"East, I think."

"Which way's east?"

"What way you come in?"

"That way!"

"That way is northeast. You want to go that way and then a little southeast when you get to the Y in the road.

Then keep to your left. It's about two miles the other side of that old barn with Red Man on the side. Red Man Chewing Tobacco. On your left. You'll see it."

There was a funny look about her: her eyes bulged, and her lips were purplish. Her directions weren't good either. He drove that way and never saw the barn, so he turned around and came back and looked for the barn on the right side, but no barn, so he headed back to Bolivia, but Bolivia wasn't there anymore. It was getting on toward noon.

It was four o'clock before he ever found the truckstop. He had a long time to think up something to tell Myrtle, but he still had no idea what to say. But she wasn't there anyway. The waitress said, "You mean the lady in the blue coat?" Florian didn't remember what color Myrtle's coat was. He wasn't sure exactly how to describe her except as *real mad*, probably. "*Ja*, that's the lady in the blue coat," she said. "Oh, she left here hours ago. Her son come to get her."

Florian sat and had a cup of coffee and a piece of apple pie. "Can you tell me the quickest way to get to Lake Wobegon from here?" he asked. "Lake what?" she said. "I never heard of it. It can't be around here."

But it was, not too far away, and once he got off the freeway he found his way straight home, although it was dark by then. He stopped at the Sidetrack for a quick bump. He felt he owed it to himself after all he'd been 5 through and what with what he was about to go through. "Where's the old lady?" asked Wally. "Home, waiting for me," he said.

He headed south and saw his house, and kept going. Carl's pickup was in the driveway and he couldn't see facing the both of them. He parked on the crossroad and sat, just beyond Roger Hedlund's farm, where he could watch his house. It was dark except a light was on in the kitchen and one in the bathroom. Roger's house was lit up. What if Roger should see him and come out to investigate? Out here in the country, a parked car stands out more than a little bit, you might as well be towing a searchlight behind you. It's considered unusual for a man to sit in his car in the evening on a crossroad an eighth of a mile from his own house, just sit there. If Roger came out, Florian thought he'd explain that he was listening to the radio and it was a Lutheran show so the old lady wouldn't have it in the house—Roger was Lutheran, he'd like that.

He ducked down as a car came slowly past, its headlights on high beam. The preacher on the radio might be Lutheran, he didn't know. It sure wasn't the Rosary. The man was talking about sinners who had wandered away from the path, and it seemed to Florian to fit the situation. "Broad is the road that leadeth to destruction, and narrow is the path of righteousness"—that seemed to be true too, from what he knew of freeways. The preacher mentioned forgiveness, but Florian wasn't sure about that.

He wondered what this preacher would do if *he* had forgotten his wife at a truckstop and gotten lost; the preacher knew a lot about forgiveness theoretically but what would he do in Florian's situation? A woman sang, "Softly and tenderly Jesus is calling, calling for you and for me. See by the portals he's waiting and watching. Calling, O sinner come home."

> Come home, come home—
> Ye who are weary come home.

Florian felt weary. Seventy-two is old to get yourself in such a ridiculous situation. He waited as long as he could for Carl to leave, and then the coffee inside him reached the point of no return and he started up the engine. Taking a leak in another man's field: he drew the line at that. He turned on his headlights, and right when he did he saw Carl's headlights far away light up and the beams swung around across the yard and Carl headed back toward town.

Florian coasted up his driveway with the headlights out. He still did not have a speech ready. He was afraid. He also had to pee. Outside, on the porch, he smelled supper: breaded fish fillets. He was surprised that the door was unlocked—they never have locked it but he thought she might if she thought he was coming.

He hung up his coat in the mud room and looked

around the corner. She was at the stove, her back to him, stirring something in a pan. He cleared his throat. She turned. She said, "Oh thank God." She dropped the spoon on the floor and ran to him on her old legs and said, "Oh Daddy, I was so scared. Oh Daddy, don't ever leave me again. I'm sorry I said what I did. I didn't mean it. I didn't mean to make you so angry at me. Don't leave me again like that."

Tears came to his eyes. To be so welcome—in his own home. He was about to tell her that he hadn't left her, he'd forgotten her; then she said, "I love you, Daddy. You know that."

He was going to tell her, but he didn't. It occurred to him that leaving her on account of passionate anger might be better than forgetting her because of being just plain dumb. There wasn't time to think this through clearly. He squeezed her and whispered, "I'm sorry. I was wrong. I promise you that I'll never do a dumb thing like that again."

She felt good at supper and put on the radio; she turned it up when she heard "The Saint Cloud Waltz." *Sometimes I dream of a mansion afar but there's no place so lovely as right where we are, here on a planet that's almost a star, we dance to the Saint Cloud Waltz.* That night he lay awake, incredulous. That she thought he was capable of running away, like a John Barrymore or something. Seventy-two years old, married forty-eight years, and she thought that maybe it hadn't worked out and he might fly the coop like people do in songs? Amazing woman. He got up at six o'clock, made scrambled eggs and sausage and toast, and felt like a new guy. She felt better too. The lump on her head felt like all the other lumps and there was no blood on her toothbrush. She said, "I wonder if I hadn't ought to call down there about that appointment." "Oh," he said, "I think by now they must know you're all right."

High Rise

It has been a quiet week in Lake Wobegon. It turned hot on Tuesday and Clarence got the Crosley electric window fan out from the basement. But it was cool in the basement, so he sat down for a while to catch up on some old magazines. 1958 was a hot year too. He brought the fan up and took the quilts down and read some more. Eisenhower: quite a man. And those tailfins. I don't believe you ever see a car in that exact shade of green these days. And white sidewalls. Do they still exist?

Questions like those keep him awake at night: Audie Murphy, alive or dead? What happened to Mary Miller of the 42nd Street Gang on "Sunday in Manhattan"? What a great show that was. It's hot and you kick off the blanket in your sleep and then you're aroused by your indecency and wake up and cover yourself and think about Mary Miller for a while and go to sleep.

There was a thin high-pitched whine in the air from clouds of mosquitoes and gnats, but we're used to that. It's summer and this is Minnesota, and mosquitoes are part of our heritage, going back to the seventeenth century when French explorers searching for the fabled oilfields of the north, canoeing through swamps and streams on the sweltering muskeg, stopped and looked at each other covered with black insects and red welts and dizzy from slapping their heads and said, "What do (you) say (we) try Quebec first and leave this for later?" And so our fabled oilfields remain safe and secure. Mosquitoes are what don't show up in the gorgeous color photographs of Minnesota, and we're not supposed to complain, but you ought to admire us for living here, it's an accomplishment, not everybody could do it.

Ella Anderson was in her garden digging up a patch of elderly irises, coated with mosquito lotion, Nuits de la Nord, which smells like ripe bananas. Father Emil was in the rectory garden putting in his onions—he has resigned as pastor of Our Lady and is only staying temporarily to help Father Wilmer get settled, but Sunday after Mass, Wilmer had his bags packed for two weeks of vacation. "How can you?" said Father. "You just started. I put in almost fifty years, I got to retire." Wilmer said he had thirty-seven vacation days coming from the diocese. Father never heard about a vacation policy. "Oh yes," Wilmer said, "and we got profit-sharing. IRAs for clergy. It's new this year." Father Emil thought, Next thing they'll have a Frequent Prayer program with prizes, put an odometer on the Rosary. So Wilmer went to San Francisco. He said, "No mosquitoes there, you know." Father Emil walked behind him out to the car, carrying

Wilmer's gym bag. "They got sharks," he said, "they got snakes, they got mad dogs come down out of the hills on hot days and bite you in the hinder, you'll be sick for a week." Wilmer just laughed. No mosquitoes in California, and that's a vacation for him. That's why Father put in his onions. Green onions are a mosquito preventative. In forty-four years, he has yet to be bitten on the lips.

"It doesn't seem right," Myrtle said to Sister Arvonne, up in the Our Lady basement, planning the picnic for the Daughters of Martha in June, "that we have the God-given beauties of nature and can't even enjoy them for the Goddamned mosquitoes, it doesn't seem fair." Myrtle is seventy-three and she has talked that way all her life. Her husband, Florian, you couldn't get a swear word out of him if you squeezed him with a pair of pliers, but Myrtle has a gland in her neck next to the thyroid that secretes profanity, especially when mosquitoes get bad. She sits in her yellow lawn chair in the shade and slaps and swears, and now she's talking about moving to a senior citizen high rise in Saint Cloud. "Mosquitoes don't go higher than the third floor unless there's an updraft. I read an article on it. You live above the sixth floor, you're free and clear.

She's campaigned for the move to the high rise for almost two years, going back to when she got in a fight with her sister-in-law Beatrice over a blue Bavarian crystal vase Beatrice chose from Myrtle's mother's things after she died. Myrtle thought it was odd to let an *in-law* pick over Mother's things but she didn't want to say anything, and then Beatrice drew the short straw and reached out and picked the one precious thing out of the lot, the blue vase that to Myrtle had been since early childhood the most beautiful object she could imagine, left by a princess as a token of a gay life to come. Saturday, when the girls cleaned the worn-out little house, they shined up the crystal vase and walked around to see the diamonds that it made from a beam of light. It was magical. Fat Beatrice clutched it to her tremendous bosom and sighed for happiness, who knew nothing about this vase, hadn't grown up with it, she could buy one in a dime store and it'd be the same to her—but Myrtle didn't want to say anything, so she hauled off and slapped her across the face hard, and Beatrice squeezed the vase and it shattered and one shard pierced her left breast. She jumped up and tore off Myrtle's wig and the other sisters fell in between them. They cried and picked up the broken glass. They said they were sure glad Mother wasn't alive to see this, it woulda killed her. They made Beatrice and Myrtle kiss and make up. Myrtle gave Beatrice a peck on the cheek and whispered into Beatrice's right ear, "Jesus goddamn you fat old bitch." Six lowdown nasty words from the mouth of a grandma. There's been a poisoned courtesy between them ever since, fourteen years of saying hello between thin hard lips, and two years ago, when Beatrice 13 became president of Catholic Mothers, Myrtle wanted to leave town.

Myrtle'd like to live someplace exciting. Lake Wobegon is boring. She almost moved to Minneapolis in 1937. She was going to go and then she didn't and she's been talking about it ever since, how she came *this close* to going and if only she had, well, she wouldn'ta ever had to put up with this horseshit. Whenever her kids were rotten, she told them how she'd almost gone away in 1937 and wished she had. She's been putting up with it for fifty years. She's sick and tired of it.

To Florian, the idea of moving to Saint Cloud is unthinkable. Myrtle says, "I seen a article in the *Times* about a new high rise opening up. We oughta get our names in for that—you know some people have to wait two years on the waiting list before they get in, that's how much people our age want to live in one, two years you got to wait. That's how desirable they are. Two years." Florian gets up to put toast in the toaster, make another cup of Sanka, stalling for time, wishing she'd forget it. "Well?" she says. "Well?"

"I just don't think it's realistic," he says. Living in a tall building, seven, eight stories up: he went up the Foshay Tower once, thirty-one stories, and couldn't stand near the edge because there was suction from the ground trying to pull him off. So if you lived on the eighth floor and couldn't go near the windows and had to walk around next to the inside wall and maybe tie your left ankle to the bedpost at night, what kind of life would it be?

He's lived there at the Krebsbach place since before he was born. His mother had him in the downstairs bedroom, presumably conceived of him there too and the six others before him, four of them dead now. The latest one, dear Ruth, his favorite sister, how funny and dear she was and yet her taste in men, my God! four husbands, the first of whom was a disaster and they went down from there. But as long as she lived and as bad as she felt, she could always come back home because Florian lived here. He rents out the land to Roger, but he still has the house and every Thanksgiving and Christmas and Memorial Day and Fourth of July there are some Krebsbachs there, depending on how they feel about each other that year.

"Give me one reason," Myrtle says, "give me one *good* reason why we wouldn't be better off in an apartment in Saint Cloud."

That's why, a few years ago, Florian started raising ducks. At first a dozen and now a flock of thirty-six.

"It's good meat," he said, "and you know, they do eat mosquitoes."

"Ducks don't eat mosquitoes, don't be dumb."

"Oh yes, they eat their weight in mosquitoes. I read that in an article."

Myrtle looks at him. What is he talking about? She's

the one who reads the articles. She never read word one about ducks.

"If they eat mosquitoes, how come we got so many we can't even sit in the backyard?"

"If they didn't eat them, we'd have a lot more, we wouldn't be able to sit, period."

Since Myrtle started talking high rise, Florian has bought a number of old Farmall tractors at auction and a corn drill and an old combine. He talks about fixing them up. Since she started talking about how nice a three-room apartment would be, he'd been picking up old dressers cheap and antique bedsteads and washstands. As an investment. And expanding his duck herd.

So when she says to give her one reason, he says, "What can I do with the ducks?"

He takes a kitchen chair and sits in the yard and all the ducks come around. He holds up the cheese curls in one hand and caramel popcorn in the other and his audience looks up and he tells them a joke. He says: So one day a duck come in this bar and ordered a whiskey and a bump and the bartender was pretty surprised, he says, "You know we don't get many of you ducks in here." The duck says, "At these prices I'm not surprised." And he tosses out the popcorn and they laugh. *Wak wak wak wak wak.*

I was shot in the leg in the war.

Have a scar?

16   *No thanks I don't smoke.*

Senator K. Thorvaldson saw Father Emil planting onions behind the rectory, he walked over and said, "I thought you were retiring and moving South."

"Well, I thought you were going to marry that woman out in Maine and move East."

"Well, maybe I will, I don't know. It's hard to leave here though when I'm so curious to see what's going to happen to you. I want to find out how the story ends before I go away."

Father mentioned Myrtle and Florian. "Telling jokes to ducks!" says Senator K. "Has Florian lost his marbles or what, then?"

"He has forgotten an awful lot of jokes but the few he remembers the ducks enjoy them over and over."

Florian sits out back and just about falls over, some of them are so good.

Hey, call me a taxi.

Okay, you're a taxi.

"Give me one reason," she says, "why we shouldn't pack up and leave this town."

He says: So this couple went to get a divorce, she was eighty-none and he was ninety-two—the judge said, "Why? You've been married seventy years and now you want a divorce?" "We hate each other," she said. "We haven't been able to stand each other since 1932." "Why did you wait so long?" he said. "We wanted to wait until the children were dead. This woulda killed them."

Lyle's Roof

It has been a quiet week in Lake Wobegon. On Tuesday Carl Krebsbach's brother-in-law Lyle tried to start his lawnmower, which had died because the grass was so high that he hadn't cut sooner because it'd rained so much, and a shingle fell off his roof. He looked up and another one slid off and almost creamed him. There was white mossy stuff on the underside of the shingles, and though it was asphalt, it was soft, like a living thing, and it crumbled in his hands. It had held on to the roof as long as it could and then it died. A dead shingle.

People have been mentioning the roof to Lyle for years, in a roundabout sort of way. You can't stand and flat tell a man his house is falling apart. Carl says, "You know, if you'd like me to, I could climb up on your roof and check some of those shingles, they look like they might be loose"—but Lyle is leery of accepting help lest the person helping him think the reason he needs help is that he's stupid.

Lyle thought he better climb up and have a look. He doesn't have a long enough ladder, and he didn't want to borrow Carl's and involve Carl, so Lyle thought he'd go to the attic and look at it from underneath. He looked for his flashlight. He had an idea he'd left it in the corner of the basement when he looked at the water pump. It was dark in there, so he couldn't see if the flashlight was there or not, and he didn't want to go in there, because he could hear water running and the pump is electrical. So he went to put in a fuse so the light would work and he could look for the flashlight. He found a couple dozen old fuses on the fusebox, waiting to be healed, and none worked, so he unscrewed one from another socket and put it in and there was screeching and screaming behind him. He turned and saw a skillsaw making sparks on the concrete floor coming straight for him, and he grabbed for the fuse and touched something that made his whole body feel for one moment like a piece of history, pulled his hand back, and the saw came to the end of its cord and yanked it and stopped. It was all quiet except for the water-pump moan—the same sound he'd gone to check on when he left the flashlight back in there. But now it was louder. And it smelled of something burning.

Five disasters in five minutes, including attempts on his life by a shingle and a skillsaw, and all on a *summer* afternoon. Now comes fall, and after that life starts to get serious. He went to start the lawnmower again and had an idea: why not dig up this sod and put it on the roof? He'd

seen that in the *National Geographic*, from Iceland or
somewhere, some cold country. If the roof could grow
moss, why not grass? People would laugh at him, but then
they laugh at him now—so what's the difference? The
difference is that, in a couple years, they'd see what a
brilliant idea it is.

He would have to give this some careful thought.

He couldn't think while mowing, so he sat down to
think in his lawn chair, and soon he was dreaming: something about green grass but not on a roof.

One man who's noticed Lyle's roof is Clarence Bunsen, who takes long early-morning walks for his heart. At
6:00 A.M., in the early light, this little town is so shining
and perfect, so fresh, so still, if you took eleventh-grade
English from Miss Heinemann you would think of
Wordsworth:

> There was a time when meadow, grove, and stream,
> The earth, and every common sight,
>   To me did seem
>   Appareled in celestial light,
> The glory and the freshness of a dream.
> It is not now as it hath been of yore;—
>   Turn wheresoe'er I may,
>   By night or day,
> The things which I have seen I now can see no more.

20

Clarence walks up Taft Street to where it becomes the road to the dump, and on mornings when he feels worse he walks farther.

This summer Bunsen Motors isn't taking in enough money to keep four people on the payroll: Clarence and Clint Bunsen, and Stanley and Earl, plus Marlys Diener doing part-time bookkeeping. They're not selling the Fords they used to. People are driving forty and fifty miles to buy a car at a big dealer, they don't have the loyalty to the home town that they used to have, and they're not even ashamed to display the foreign dealer's nameplate on the trunk: there it is, big as sin, *Ogilvie Toyota, Saint Cloud*. Who is Ogilvie? Does he go to the Lutheran church? Does he go to any church? They don't know him. For all they know, he could be in Las Vegas, running around with showgirls and eating spoonfuls of cocaine; meanwhile, Clarence, their neighbor and friend, who if they were suddenly in deep water he'd be there to help, is in some fairly deep water of his own. He's got to borrow seven thousand dollars to get through September. Wednesday he saw parked in front of the Chatterbox a brand-new red Ford Bronco 2 that Harold Diener, husband of Marlys, had bought in Minneapolis. Clarence was sick. It broke his heart. But he tried not to show it. He admired the car. "That's nice, Harold," he said. "That's real good. Four-wheel drive. That'll be handy when win- 21 ter comes. You sure know your cars, Harold. I oughta hire you as a salesman."

> The rainbow comes and goes,
> And lovely is the rose;
> The moon doth with delight
> Look round her when the heavens are bare;
> Waters on a starry night
> Are beautiful and fair;
> The sunshine is a glorious birth;
> But yet I know, where'er I go,
> That there hath passed away a glory from the earth.

You live in a small town, you learn about people. You learn that certain people, if they say they'll be there to teach school on Tuesday, they'll be there, and some people won't, and if you call them up Tuesday evening, they'll say, "Oh, you meant *this* Tuesday." It's always the same ones who are prompt and faithful and dependable, and if they're ten minutes late you should call the police, and always the same others who say, "Are you sure today is Tuesday? But yesterday was—Oh yeah, it was Monday, wasn't it? Well . . . do you still need me?"

School started on Tuesday and suddenly it became awful quiet. All the air went out of the tire, the kids disappeared with their goofy ideas and dumb jokes and there
was nothing left downtown but business, and not much of

that. There was hardly a car on Main street, you would've had to wait around to get in a traffic accident. At Krebsbach Chev, Florian was in a dark mood. Clarence came up and poured himself a cup of coffee, and Florian got ready to say, "Whatcha put cream in coffee for? Ruins it. I thought only women did that." But Clarence took his black, leaned against the parts counter, and said, "Jeez, what a week. Only Tuesday and it feels like Friday. I'll bet I don't sell one car."

That afternoon, at a quarter of four, Florian stepped out of the Chatterbox Cafe and turned to his left to go up to the garage. As he turned, he heard wheels behind him. He looked back and there was the Best boy coming on fast on his ten-speed. Florian ducked to his left, the Best boy went to his right, and they crashed. Florian fell over and the boy landed a little ways away. Florian sat up, making sure he was not killed, and asked, "Are you all right?"

The boy waited for Florian to yell at him and, when Florian didn't, went home to be yelled at by his folks for riding on the sidewalk and knocking down an old man, but they didn't either, and at school on Wednesday he was still waiting to be yelled at. He thought that perhaps Florian would be the speaker at assembly and talk about bike safety. He was sure Florian would write a letter to the editor—"I was walking along the sidewalk one day last week when one of our grade-school boys attempted to 23 kill me. Isn't it time we stop coddling these vicious children and start putting some of them behind bars as an example to the others?"

The reason he didn't get yelled at is, ever since Florian forgot Myrtle at the truckstop on their way to the Cities, he's expected something to happen to him, and being knocked down by a bike was much easier than other things he imagined.

It's a primitive sense of justice: you do bad, and your Creator smacks you one—but there it is. One day you're daydreaming at the wheel, you smash into someone's rear end. She gets out of her car, looks at the busted taillight, and smiles. She's relieved; she says, "Well, it could've been a lot worse." You've just run into a guilty person. She did something in the past twenty-four hours that made her think the universe would land on her with both feet. She'd be covered with boils, wrapped in burlap, sitting in the ashes, flies on her, and ligthning coming closer and closer, but all it is is a taillight. Not bad. She smiles and drives away. Now *you* start to feel guilty. Days later, the Best boy is still hearing footsteps, waiting for the big hand to grab him and spin him around and the voice to say, "Why you—"

Sometimes it's hard to get into trouble in this little town. There was an old guy years ago got so depressed he decided to kill himself, and he got a flask of whiskey and went down to the lake to throw himself in and drown. But he couldn't cut a hole in the ice. It had been a cold winter. He had some whiskey and he banged on the ice with his ax but couldn't cut a hole. He had more whiskey, and then he opened up a hole big enough to stick his hand in, and he drank the rest of the whiskey and took off all his clothes except his boots. He hiked off naked into the dim winter night and felt sleepy and then heard voices—women, he thought—and was scared he'd be seen and ran back and got his clothes on. He went home, slept, and woke up with a hangover worse than death and was resurrected from the hangover and decided to live. That's a true story from long ago. I believe it's true, except about the boots, but he died in 1978, so it's too late to check.

It rained more this week, a heavy rain that fell straight down, and eventually Lyle found his flashlight and looked up in the attic under the roof, which has been leaking for a long time into the plastic buckets in his daughter's bedroom, and he was astounded how awful it looked. Not just wet but slimy, slippery, like a place where mutant creatures come from, shiny green things with empty eyes reaching out for us. For two years Carl has told him he ought to fix his roof, which made Lyle furious but it also made Lyle nervous because Carl knows about these things. Lyle teaches science at the high school; he knows about the stratosphere, the ecosphere, the atmosphere, genetics, the cosmos, but not about roofs.

He climbed down from the attic, and he went downstairs to the furnace room and poured himself a stiff drink. No ice cubes or soda down there, just the bottle in the workbench. He wondered what to do. He didn't want to ask Carl for help, he was tired of him helping, of coming home from school and finding his brother-in-law had got his sink apart—*Lyle's sink*. He had another drink. Poor kids, living in a house that might fall down on their heads because their dad doesn't know what to do.

He felt like going to bed but he went up to the bedroom and called someone. He took the phone to the end of the cord, took it into the closet, sat down on a pile of shoes, and tried to disguise his voice to make it sound sober.

"Father? Is this Father Conway? This is Lyle. You don't know me but I live up here in Lake Wobegon, and I hate to bother you with something like this but I can't talk to my priest about it, it's something I've been embarrassed about for a long time—Yes? Well, I appreciate your saying that. I do. I'll try. It's just hard to find the words to say what I've been going through over this, but, anyway, it's about my roof.

"No, I said 'roof.' It's my roof. The roof on my house.'"

There's a story about Lyle's house, as there is about most houses in town. That's why old people walk so slow, because they're remembering all the stories. I'm not that old but I know a lot because I used to hang out with old people back when there used to be real old people. Now everyone is sort of my age or younger, and most people don't know much more than I do. It's disappointing to become a leading authority in the field when you still have so much you want to learn. But I do know that Lyle's house was built in 1889 by a carpenter named Swanson who started a milling business to make door and window frames.

He was tall and sported a fine black mustache and had three daughters who worshipped the ground he walked on, and after he died, they lived in the house, adoring his memory. When they got old, about thirty years ago, they couldn't bear the thought of anybody else ever living in their father's fine house. An ordinary two-story wood frame house to everyone else, but to them it was their father's realm, the embodiment of his life and wisdom and goodness, and they wrote in their will that, after the last of them deceased, the house would be torn down.

Then they died: one, two, three, close together. Each death seemed to drain the life from the survivors, and the family collapsed, and a few weeks later, the heir to their estate, a nephew, the son of their ne'er-do-well brother, young Victor rode into town, his long black hair combed high on his head, and a lawyer at his side, to claim what was rightfully his. The entire town came to despise both of them within twenty-four hours. The town couldn't decide which one they despised more. People had never agreed on anything so unanimously and heartily as that 27 young Victor was despicable, heartless, and deserved to be cheated, and they set out to deprive him of that house.

The sisters' will provided that, if the house wasn't torn down within sixty days, then he wouldn't inherit the rest of the estate, about forty thousand dollars in cash in the First Ingqvist State Bank. The town didn't want to see the house torn down. It was a nice house, and if Victor didn't tear it down, the forty thousand dollars went to the library. Victor said it was his house and he started to rip the roof off. The town council made him stop while they studied the matter, looking through the municipal ordinances hoping that their forefathers in their wisdom might have passed something usable that they could hammer him with, and found an odd little law, passed in 1889 that said that the demolition of a building must be completed within fourteen days. Victor had torn some roof off about five days before, and it was a week until the next council meeting. That left two days to tear it down in, and one of those days was a Sunday, so all he had was one day.

He did his best. He arrived early and his lawyer with him, with crowbars and big hammers, but his grandfather had built the house better than he knew, and by noon Victor could see he wasn't going to make it. He'd made a lot of dents in it, busted windows, beat the dust out of it, pried off some boards, but he wasn't going to be able to 28 level it by nightfall, and so he would lose forty thousand dollars. He started to yell and run around like a madman, which meant he got even less done. His lawyer saw that he wouldn't get paid and turned quiet and gloomy, and Victor went to pieces. He yelled out the window: "I'll give you two thousand dollars to help me tear my house down!"

A little gang of men stood out in the dusty street. They seemed interested, so he made another offer: "I'll give you three thousand dollars to help me tear my house down."

"Would that be per man or for the whole bunch of us?"

"Three thousand dollars apiece."

"Could we see some of that first?"

So the sun went down and he left town and the bank sold the house to Lyle: a good house, well built, but one that had sustained some violence, so he has problems with his plumbing, his wiring, his drainage, his roof, that other people might not have. And he has a problem with three ghosts who don't feel good about him being there.

He talked to Father Conway for about an hour—about roofs but also about football and about fall and what a fine season it is. Lyle went off to work the next day to talk about the quiet but passionate life of amoeba, but at noon Mr. Halvorson asked if he could give up his lunch period and take Miss Peterson's speech class—she had had lunch and went home sick—and Lyle said, Sure.

He walked into the speech room and smelled intense fear. Twenty people seventeen years old sat in three rows, facing a low platform. Fifty-five minutes in the class period, each student to speak impromptu for three minutes about himself or herself, so there'd be no more than eighteen speeches, so two would escape till the next day, and of the twenty, about sixteen were hoping to be one of the two.

An impromptu speech about yourself . . . "Well, what is there to say?" one boy said. "I don't know. I was born and I have a family, of course, and I'm in school and—I don't know, what am I supposed to talk about?"

"Just tell us about yourself," Lyle said from the back.

"But there isn't anything important to tell."

"Let us decide that. Just talk about whatever comes to mind."

"What if nothing comes to mind?"

There were terrible silences when a speaker froze in midsentence and the audience looked down out of decency, studied their fingernails, while the poor person took a deep trembling breath. Lyle sat in back, and a few feet away, his daughter Mary. He began to feel ill himself. Finally it was her turn and she stood up, her face red, and he closed his eyes and put his head in his hands. *Ah, youth.*

"I was born in 1969," she said, "in Minneapolis. We were there visiting some relatives, I guess. I don't know—I wasn't there, of course." Laughter. Silence. Lyle remembered that weekend when she was born, and tears came to his eyes.

"My first memory is of a day when we had a blanket on the grass and my mother and dad and I were sitting on it—I don't know where this was, but the sun was shining and dogs were barking far away, and I had this feeling—and I guess I've always felt this—that my family was very close to me, always near, even when they were gone, so I've never really been that afraid. Not even now."

In his head, Lyle heard a voice, and it said, "Lyle, now have your roof fixed. Keep your house in order."

The bell rang. The two who didn't give speeches let out their breaths and relaxed, not knowing that one thing worse than giving a speech is thinking about giving a speech. Lyle went to the office and called Carl. "Carl?" he said. "Uh, I was wondering if you had any time free tonight to come over and have a look upstairs—I've decided I really ought to go ahead on that roof project and not pursue some of these other options I was considering, so I think we ought to get it down before it snows."

January

It was cold—got down to thirty-some below a couple
nights, according to old guys who get up to pee—so that
when Lyle turned the key in the ignition, his blue Impala
gave a low moan, like Roland Park in *Blood on the Saddle*
when he saved Don Decatur's life by jumping between
him and the outlaw ambush at the Little Crazy River and
lay in the tumbleweeds and Don said, "Take it easy. Don't
try to talk. You're going to be all right," but you knew
Roland was a goner when he let out that moan. Then he
sagged in Don's arms and went limp. So there was no
getting around it: the car was dead.

She was a good car. Lyle bought her in 1978, six years
old but in terrific shape thanks to Virginia Ingqvist's fear
of driving after she totaled a previous Chevy, even Lyle's
brother-in-law Carl Krebsbach, a shrewd man about cars,
agreed that Lyle got a heck of a good deal. Lyle just
didn't have the knack of starting her up on cold mornings. His tendency was to get angry and flood the carburetor. Of course he had jumper cables, like everybody else,
but that required a live car to start his deadster, most
likely Carl's next door, and Lyle cringed at the thought of

asking. Carl's Chevy pickup roared to life every morning; Lyle heard it as he shaved, and sometimes he nicked himself. It made a sound like "nonagenarian-rn-rn-rn." Carl gunned it a few times—in a boastful way, Lyle thought, like a lion roaring after intercourse. And then Carl would come over, let himself into the kitchen, pour a cup of coffee, and offer to start Lyle's. Or he said, "Where's your keys?" and just went out and did it. "Don't bother, I don't need the car today," Lyle said, "I feel like walking," but Carl believed a car should be started in cold weather whether you drove it or not.

Sometimes Carl poked his head in the garage as Lyle stood at the side of his dead pal. Carl opened the hood and fiddled with the carburetor, and said, "Here, let me try it," and the car picked up its head and started. Maddening. An impossible problem, you're resigned to it, and then a cheerful guy reaches over casually with one hand and solves it. Lyle is the science teacher at the high school, he can explain cold, but he can't accept it, having grown up in Torrance, California. He's lived in Minnesota since 1971, a transplant that didn't take. Even now, when December rolls around and the first blizzard rolls in from Montana as regular as the North Coast Limited, he looks out the window and wonders, "What's going on here? What's the matter?" And when it's thirty below, he feels that something is definitely wrong. Then cool Carl shows up in his immense parka and insulated rubber boots and a big grin on his face and says, "It's a cold one. Boy, I think we mighta set a record."

Carl has the golden touch. Once Carl caught a walleye off Art's Point that raced toward the boat and leaped almost into Carl's arms. Landed in the boat, and later when Carl cleaned him he found an Indian-head penny, a high school ring (class of 1954, which was Carl's class), and a piece of tinfoil off a bottle of pink champagne *that Carl himself had drunk*. Late one night in 1955, trying to get over the girl he had given his ring to who had told him to get lost. She took the ring off her necklace and threw it in the lake. "There. Go get it," she said. Carl was heartbroken. He returned to the spot with his champagne, got drunk, couldn't remember what he had done with the foil. Now he knew. Both had come back to him by way of a tremendous fish as a sign that his life would be happy. He kept the ring and the penny and threw the foil back in the lake, for more good luck. "I've got the ring right here if you want to see it," he told Lyle. It fit him perfectly. Lyle was amazed. "And the fish?" he asked. "In the freezer," Carl said. He looked straight at Lyle: "Now that's what I call fishing."

Once a deer walked up behind Carl as he stood in the woods the first Saturday of deer-hunting season, waiting for a deer. ("You know that road about a hundred yards beyond Winkler's? Little dirt road heads west off the gravel? Well, you go beyond that and to your right you'll see a road goes east, just a couple ruts in the weeds. You follow that into the woods and it comes to a foundation where this guy is supposed to have lived with a Chippewa woman who was a faith healer. She could talk it right out of people, TB, cancer, heal broken bones, anything, but he was jealous and he killed her and he set fire to the house and burned himself up. You can't miss the foundation, there's an old rusted-out woodstove sitting in the middle of it—you go beyond that and there's a path goes between two chestnut trees and up the hill. You can see the water tower from the hill. You head in the opposite direction and you come down into a ravine. It's an old creek bed. That's where I was.") He was waiting for his deer when he felt a cold nose touch his hand. He did the standing broad jump, bounced off a birch tree, turned around and saw the deer. A doe, a big one. His first thought was that she had escaped from the Pet-the-Tame-Deer Park on Highway 10, and his second was that his three cousins from Minneapolis were near by who he left because he was nervous being around them the way they carried their rifles. Eugene had a way of gesturing with his that gave Carl the willies: "I'll go this way and you head up *there*" and jabbed the thing and the muzzle was looking straight at Carl's gut. Carl knocked it away and grabbed Eugene's jacket and called him an idiot. Eugene's brothers, Dave and Nick, thought Carl was being harsh. Carl walked away from them. Now he thought he didn't want to be near anything that moved, with the cousins around God knows where, and especially not a deer. He walked away, she followed. He turned and clapped, but evidently she'd been trained to come when someone clapped. He ran a little ways down the ravine and up the bank to the edge of a meadow, she had no trouble keeping up. He lay down in the tall grass, hoping she'd get bored and go away, but she stood and looked down at him with her big brown eyes. *Git! Go on! Shoo! Haw!* He was afraid she'd step on him and break his arm. That'd be a good on: "How'd you break your arm, Carl?" "Deer stepped on it." "Oh, where were you?" "In the woods, deer hunting." The deer nuzzled his pockets. He gave her half of a Salted Nut Roll. He said, "Look, it's not supposed to be this way." He felt like he was in a Walt Disney cartoon. She stood over him, drooling Nut Roll, her front legs straddling his leg, looking down at him. ("Her face was as close as yours is to mine, and I've seen deer before but not like this one, her eyes looked almost human. And then I knew what I had to do. I didn't want to but I had to. So I got up and did it before I changed my mind.")

"You didn't," Lyle said.

"Of course I did. She didn't have anything going for her, nothing. No fear. She wouldn't run. She was just as trapped as if she was hitched to a tree. If she walked up to my cousins, they'd shoot her of course but they'd hit her in the rear end, and *then* she'd run, and she'd crawl off in the bushes and die for the rest of the day. I shot her in the back of the head and she dropped like a stone, she didn't even twitch. I cleaned her and carried her to the truck. I gave her to the Dieners. I couldn't see eating her myself. And I never went hunting with those jerks again."

This seemed brutal to Lyle, but also possibly heroic. The sureness of it. *He knew what he had to do and he got up and did it before he changed his mind.* But also brutal. He asked Carl how it felt, what were his feelings at the time. Carl said, "I don't know what you mean."

Lyle asked his sister-in-law Margaret one day if she was ever worried that Carl might go over the edge. Lyle had read about guys who suddenly went crazy with a shotgun, which he didn't mention to her, not wanting to alarm her, but he thought Carl was possibly the type.

She said, "He went over the edge when he met me."

One fine day in 1957 they went to see *Dracula* at the Alhambra, which she had seen before, and right when the French doors were open in the young woman's boudoir, the curtains blowing in, the mist rolling up from the moors, the bat flew in, and suddenly Dracula was bending over the bed—right then she leaned over and kissed Carl on the neck.

She had thought of Carl as a calm fellow until then. In fact, it was one of her few remaining doubts about him as a husband, that he might be too calm. Other faults she 37 had improved. He smoked so much at first he smelled like burnt toast and his hair oil was 10W-30, and she changed all that and also helped him learn to eat food and converse at the same time, quite a trick for a boy from a big family whose only sound at dinner was rhythmic chewing and swallowing. It was hard getting him to say much, though, and she wondered if he might be a little on the dull side, a man with nerves of wood, until she kissed him on the neck and found out that he had deep reserves of nervous energy. In one second, he distributed the box of popcorn over six rows of seats.

To Lyle, winter was frightening. He woke up cold in the morning. Somehow he and Janice didn't make enough heat together, and then there was the slab of ice on the window that got thicker every day. It was too cold to get out the ladder and put on the storm window, and besides Carl might see him and come over and do it right. As he pulled on his pants (the floor was cold, too), he thought about the plumbing. They kept a trickle dripping out of each faucet at night to prevent frozen pipes, but you never could tell. A good pipe freeze could run a guy a few hundred bucks for new plumbing. Stumbling downstairs, he thought he caught the smell of dead car in the air. He cranked the thermostat up to eighty, and down below the old furnace creaked and throbbed in its bowels and shook like a dog shitting a peach pit. One day it too would die

and what would he do then? He was in debt for ten other

things already, including his wife's orthodontist, a mealy-mouthed guy she met at a Catholic Action meeting who talked her into getting braces (they were cold, too). He owed money on the Chev (deceased). It'd be a cold day in hell before the bank would give him more, a schoolteacher with four kids and a wife with braces and a chickenfeed salary.

In November, everything starts to go downhill, and you can't stop it, it's going to slide as far as it's going to slide. Lyle's philosophy of winter. Nature out of control. What scared him sometimes was the thought that others might be affected even more than he—Carl? Maybe not. Maybe an older gent, living alone, "a very quiet nice man" the dumb neighbors would tell police when it was all over, the sudden sniper attack from an upstairs window, the quiet old psychopath picking off children with his .22 as they trudged home in the twilight. A man did that once, maybe in North Dakota. He was innocent on grounds of being wacko. There were a number of little houses in town whose windows were dark. Who lived there and what was going through their minds? In the olden days, minds snapped in winter like twigs and the authorities sent wagons out to the small towns and farms to round up cases for the asylum, so what was—And then he heard the kitchen door open. Big boots and a jingle of keys. "Hey!" he yelled. The door slammed. By the time he got 39 to the kitchen, he heard his car start up. Carl revved it a couple times.

"That's hard on the carburetor," Lyle thought. He went upstairs to take a shower so he wouldn't have to thank him.

Eloise

It has been a quiet week in Lake Wobegon. It was warm and bright and the trees were in full color, magnificent, explosive, like permanent fireworks—reds and yellows, oranges, some so brilliant that Crayola never put them in crayons for fear the children would color outside the lines. Maple trees the color of illicit romance, blazing red sumac and oaks and aspen, such color that you weren't sure you were in this world but perhaps had stepped through a seam in the tapestry and walked into a magical wood. But the only trail through there is a cowpath, so you have to watch where you step.

Florian and Myrtle Krebsbach went driving Tuesday to look at the beautiful trees, which neither of them enjoys, but they go because they've done it for years. Myrtle gets carsick more easily now since she bumped her head on the cupboard. The bright colors only made her dizziness more vivid. Florian was grumpy because he hates to see the odometer roll on his '66 Chev (like new, only forty-seven thousand miles on her). Low mileage is a form of youth to Florian, it means plenty of mileage to come. He drove slowly toward Millet and back and Myrtle hung on to the strap. She said, of the fall colors, "Well, if this don't prove to them there's an Almighty, I don't know what in hell will." They drove 6.2 miles at twenty-five mph and returned to home base, where he wiped the engine clean with a rag soaked in gasoline. The smell of gas makes Florian perk up.

The leaves reached their peak about Thursday and then, in late afternoon, seemed to dim. Friday morning we woke up and could see that we had passed our apex and were heading for the nadir.

It was still warm, though, so when Ranger Steve came to the third grade with a boxful of snakes, they were pretty lively. Snakes are our friends, not slimy, not evil, but really very beautiful and nothing to be afraid of, he said. "I'm sure Mrs. Hughes isn't afraid of snakes—look," he said, and draped a black one on her shoulder as her body shrank and then stiffened. "See? Snakes aren't slimy at all. Actually their skin is rather dry—right, Mrs. Hughes? This is called a bridle snake; it bites, but only if you bother it."

Ranger Steve smiled. "It's all right, there's nothing to worry about," he said to Mrs. Hughes, whose eyes were shut, and took the snake in his big manly hand, and set it on his broad shoulder. Instantly the harmless reptile dove into the V of his collar and disappeared. Ranger Steve said, *"Oh God,"* and grabbed at it. He was wearing a green jump suit, with no belt for a roadblock, and he turned his back to the children and bent over and tried to grab the bridle snake in the jump suit. It was warm under there and the snake was excited, and the children heard a cry, and Steve staggered and the snake came out his left pants leg. They all helped catch it. Steve talked more about snakes but his smile had slipped to the side and gone out of focus. The passage of the bridle snake through the jump suit had worn him out, the exertion of being cool and hysterical at the same time.

Afterward, some of the boys did an imitation of Ranger Steve with the snake in his pants, and Mrs. Hughes said, "I don't consider that one bit funny," even though it was hilarious.

That's what wears out a grown-up person: the contradictions.

After school, a girl from the third grade jumped on her old blue coaster bike and tore off toward the woods to find snakes and put them on her brothers. Then, coasting down Branch Street, she saw her little brother standing looking at their dog Fatso lying by the tree, covering him up with leaves. She swerved and headed straight for the innocent little child and yelled, "I can't stop! No brakes! I can't stop," but he stood there like a stone so she stopped. She said, "You coulda been killed. Why'ntcha move? That was a close call, y'know" Fatso stood up and tottered around back of the tree but the little boy was too scared to move. "You're dumb, you know that? You're as 43 dumb as a dog." Fatso blinked. The little boy's eyes filled with tears to hear his sweet sister talk to him like that, two pools of pale-blue tears in his blue eyes, and then he made a decision that certainly changed his life: he took one step toward her with his left foot and with his right he kicked the big jerk in her ankle as hard as he could. He held back nothing. A swift hard kick.

More happened then: she chased him, caught him, threw him down, pounded him. But it wasn't important. He had done something. (The wrong thing—it's wrong to kick your sister—but sometimes the wrong thing is exactly the right thing to do.) His mother ran out and hauled her off him. "What is going on out here?"

"He kicked me—here," said Amy, and to show how much it hurt, her big brown eyes filled up with tears.

"What did you do to him?"

"Nothing. I was riding my bike."

"Paul! How could you do a thing like that?"

He looked up at his mother. He wasn't sure.

"Just for that, you come inside."

That was fine with him. He preferred inside.

These are Florian and Myrtle Krebsbach's grandchildren and their daughter Eloise, who lives around the corner from Carl. She's got three kids, these two plus a tall lonesome boy named Charlie, one in a long tradition of tall skinny lonesome boys who grew up there. Eloise's name is Best. She married Chuck Best out of high school, a handsome friendly boy, and three years ago he decided he'd been married long enough to her. He came home to pack his bags.

Eloise cried and then, when he went to the garage for his golf clubs, she locked him out of the house without so much as a warm jacket. She told him she was going to give all his clothes to the church clothing drive. When he asked for his car keys she laughed at him through the letter slot. "You want to start over, then *start* over," she said. "Don't be such a drip. This isn't a halfway house, mister, this is my home. You want to go away, go ahead, but don't ask me to give you a ride."

This took place on Greener Avenue South in Minneapolis one bright summer day in 1983. The neighbors were out working on their yards, and when they noticed the Bests' conversation—the shouts from the slot, the man in the blue blazer and tan slacks saying, "Please. Ellie. Try to control yourself"—the neighbors shut off their mowers and got busy doing quiet things. They studied trees for signs of drought, snipped at a hedge with silent little snips, quietly pulled crabgrass.

"Ellie, please. Let's discuss this. Let me in and let's talk."

"I am talking!" she said and called him a bunch of words that moms don't use. "All right," he said. "That's it. That's all I'm going to take from you." And he walked gravely and respectably down the walk. He stood at the 45 end of his walk, glancing left and right, then turned left as she opened the door and yelled, "You . . . are a . . . lousy lover!" Her voice echoed off the frame and brick houses—"lousylousylousylousyloverlousyloverloverlover" —far up the pleasant street where they'd had a sweet comfortable ten years, and he heard the lawn sprinklers whisper, "It's true, it's true, it's true, it's true."

More happened then. He came after her with excellent legal talent and pounded her pretty hard in court, and she wound up in a two-bedroom tumble-down stucco house in Lake Wobegon, where, well—to be a single woman with three children, you might as well paint the house chartreuse and convert to Islam and make it complete.

Her mother, Myrtle, says, "Eloise, you're the first one in this family ever to collect a welfare check, it's a disgrace. People talk about us. Do you know that? They never useta, and now you can hear em all over town."

She said, "Mother, don't get too ashamed now, because I've got a long way to go."

"I don't see why you can't get yourself a job."

"I'm trying."

"Try harder."

So last Thursday her little ad appeared in the *Herald-Star*. Harold himself called her Sunday and asked, "Is this legit?" So there it was: "Dancing Taught in My Home or Yours. Individual lessons. Polka, Waltz, Foxtrot, or Lindy. Eloise Krebsbach Best."

Ella Anderson called her Thursday night. "Ellie," she said, "I didn't know you could dance."

"Well, Ella, you never asked me."

"I wonder if this wouldn't help my bad hip."

Ella is old and has a hard life taking care of herself and Henry. People don't visit them, because they're embarrassed to see him, a man once important in our town, now old and sleepy. Suddenly he'll sit up and talk about your horse and somebody named David and where did the girls go? The girls went away and became middle-aged a long time ago. Ella is lonely. Her daughter Charlotte called one night and suddenly said, "Well? Mother? Do you want to or not?" And Ella couldn't remember the question. Charlotte said, "Just say yes or no," and Ella said, "Yes." And now she wonders what she said yes to.

"What's it like to be old?" Ellie asked her.

"Old age is like birds in the winter. It's hard to keep going. But you still have your good days, and one good day makes you want to keep on. I used to get so upset if any little thing went wrong. Now everything goes wrong and it doesn't bother me, and some little thing is so wonderful—if my son writes me a letter, that's wonderful. And if he puts in a picture of my grandchildren, then that's just about everything."

Ellie rolled up the old rag rug and pushed back the coffee table and chairs. "What'll it be, a waltz?" she said. A waltz it was, the "Blue Skirt Waltz," and if you walked by 47 on Thursday night and saw in the window two women dancing, one with white hair and the other with red, smiling, turning, would you have thought it was strange? Would you have stopped? Or would you have walked on, taking the sweetness of it to heart on a fall night turning cold, the bright colors, magnificence and glory all around us everywhere in the air.

Homecoming

It has been a quiet week in Lake Wobegon. It was Homecoming on Friday, the Leonards vs. Bowlus Friday night at Bowlus—an away game, on account of Leonard Field has developed a sinkhole about ten feet in diameter that suddenly sank two feet between the ten- and twenty-yard lines, not that the team used that part of the field very often. Coach Magendanz and Mr. Halvorson decided to fill it with clay, and found that filling it made it sink deeper, and removing the fill made it deeper yet. So they are keeping the hole under observation and Homecoming had to be moved to another location.

The parade was in town, though, and the Homecoming dance last night, reigned over by Queen Carla and King Jim, royalty elected by the senior class under the supervision of Mrs. Hoffarth, who eliminates inappropriate candidates. The drawback of secret ballots is the tendency on the part of a few to vote for the wrong person when nobody is looking, and once a girl other than the Queen got more votes for Queen, but those were not informed votes. The voters didn't know what Mrs. Hoffarth knew, or else they didn't have the best interests of Lake Wobegon High

School at heart. The girl in question had been to the gravel pit, parked in a car with a boy and drinking beer, and Mrs. Hoffarth maintains that when you've been to the gravel pit, you shouldn't expect to wear a tiara and ride a convertible down Main Street. A Queen should be above gravel-pit business. "If you climb down off the pedestal, don't expect to climb back up," she says. "A pedestal is not an elevator."

For years, ever since I was in school, because Mrs. Hoffarth's brother Gerald is a colonel of the National Guard, the Homecoming Queen has ridden on a Sherman tank borrowed from the Fighting 308th armory in Freeport. She rides in the forward hatch, below the cannon, and a squad of Guardsmen march in front of her. It made a deep impression on me to see a beautiful classmate in a pink gown smiling and waving from a tank and may have warped my feelings about women, particularly beautiful ones. I talk to them and hear bolts slam in the carbines and combat boots scrape on the pavement. Fear of death isn't the best basis for a friendship. It's an okay basis, but not the best. But that is personal stuff I never told anyone, so keep it under your hat—I don't want to be asked about it by every amateur psychiatrist in town. It's a little odd thing in my makeup that comes from coming where I'm from, no stranger than thinking about death every time you put on clean underwear, one of 50 those quirks a person can live with.

What's hard to live with is not the trash floating in your head but the ordinary facts of life: mortality, knowing that you'll die, and frailty, knowing that when we've got it figured out we don't, and indignity, knowing that if we manage to put up a good front we still have the backstage view. I suppose that's why I don't go home for Homecoming. They know stories about me that I can't explain away and call me by a nickname that I left home in order to lose. Wild horses couldn't drag it out of me now. But I'll tell you: it was Foxfart.

The Queen of Homecoming, Carla Krebsbach, has no odd nicknames to escape, no humiliating secrets, and she made a terrific Queen. She looked like a million dollars, wearing a white spangled dress you could get married in if you wanted, but with a dress like that, why get married and ruin your good looks? The soft contacts made her eyes glisten. She had her hair cut so her posture is improved. When Mrs. Hoffarth walked slowly across the stage holding up the tiara and the other four girls in line squeezed their eyes shut, Carla looked straight ahead, as if she knew for a fact whose head was going to be crowned. Hers. When it was, she didn't cry or hop up and down, she looked as if she was *ready.* The tiara dropped on her and it fit like Cinderella's glass slipper. She blinked and smiled a smile you could feel in the back row of the auditorium.

Unfortunately, her dad, Carl, couldn't be there to see

it. He was at his folks' house, Mrytle and Florian's, south of town, looking into the matter of their septic tank, which had reached an emergency status the night before. Florian noticed a problem last week when he raised the extension ladder and climbed up to install storm windows. He climbed up seven rungs and was only two feet off the ground. The lawn was soft as a trampoline, and the ladder sank down into it. "Well, it'll freeze soon, and then I can get around to it," he thought, but it didn't freeze soon enough. Thursday morning the ground around the ladder had sunk three feet. "Well," he thought, "these things happen." He could put in roses there. A sunken garden. Be quite attractive. Friday morning the toilet overflowed, an event that he dared not overlook. So he called Carl.

People often call Carl in this sort of situation. It's what comes from being handy. Sometimes he envies the incompetent. He inspected the sinkhole, went back to town and borrowed the backhoe from Bud, and came back and started digging.

Even he was surprised by what he found. It appeared at first to be—and as he went deeper it actually turned out to be—a 1937 Chevy coupe that someone had buried there to use as a septic tank. Whether they couldn't afford a concrete one or just had a low opinion of that car, there it was in its subterranean glory, the roof caved in, the pas- senger compartment pretty well loaded to capacity.

You'll notice how gracefully I tell this story, slipping elegantly around the unnecessary or too-vivid details, touching only the high points, but I must tell you that Carl moved the backhoe around upwind and went at it from there. It had to come out—that was the only spot for a new tank unless he wanted to cut down two oak trees or put a new tank uphill of the house, which isn't the textbook way—so he hauled out this monstrosity, getting more and more curious to know who had put it there. Florian has owned the place since Carl's grandpa died. Florian had gone to town with Myrtle to watch Homecoming. Carl loaded the Chevy onto a hay wagon and didn't bother to tie it down: if it fell off, it fell off. He hitched up to the tractor and started his lonely drive to the dump, on the other side of town. By then he was not in a good humor. "Honor thy father and thy mother," yes, but did it include this? Hauling away thirty years of family history? The Chevy septic tank had lost most of its load but with the wind at his back it was suffocating.

That may have been why he didn't ask himself why so many cars were parked along McKinley Street. He didn't see a soul around and figured the coast was clear—he wasn't getting much oxygen to his brain, only the fumes of his heritage. He chugged past the high school and the Lutheran church and had to make a right turn to get the wind off his back, because now his eyes were full of tears. 53

He hung an emergency right onto Main Street, and suddenly he was a feature attraction.

The entire population was lined up three deep on either side of Main between McKinley and Taft, and straight ahead and coming his way was the marching band and the tank behind it. The other tank.

He imagined he could make it to Taft and turn left and avoid the parade, but the old Farmall didn't have much acceleration with that load of Chev, and he and the National Guard put on the brakes and met nose to nose directly in front of the Chatterbox Cafe. The band had melted away to the side. About half the crowd began to move off toward a more distant vantage point, and the other half followed them. A strong aroma of Chev got in the ventilator of the Cafe, and the patrons silently put down their forks and emerged from the rear. Queen Carla sat on the front of the tank, her eyes almost level with her father's where he sat, in front of the old family heirloom. "How could you do this to me?" Her lips formed the words.

She was a Queen. When Queen Victoria once noticed pieces of toilet paper floating in the Thames and asked what they were, one of her counselors, the privy counselor perhaps, said, "Madam, those are printed notices saying that swimming is forbidden." Rank has its privileges, and one of them is ignorance.

The tank couldn't turn around there, the sergeant told

Carl, so he had to turn the tractor and wagon. Backward and forward, backward and forward, back and up and back, and now people were cheering and clapping. First gear, reverse, first, reverse, first, reverse. Damn. Damn. Damn. Damn. "If this falls off," he thought, "I'm going to leave it and leave town." The band began to play again, "Anchors Aweigh." When the Farmall got turned around, the band fell in behind it and the three units paraded north to the statue of the Unknown Norwegian, where the second and third units turned left. The Unknown watched the Krebsbach float chug off to the dump.

In a way, it was the most memorable Homecoming ever. Graduates who heard about it later wished they had been there, because of course it won't be repeated. It was a one-time event. Which was how Carl looked at it hours later, when he'd taken a bath and was sitting in the Sidetrack enjoying a cold Wendy's. He said, "Well, if it had to happen, I'm glad it happened where everyone could see it." That's how I feel. Who needs dignity when you can be in show business?

FOR THE BEST IN PAPERBACKS, LOOK FOR THE

In every corner of the world, on every subject under the sun, Penguin represents quality and variety—the very best in publishing today.

For complete information about books available from Penguin—including Puffins, Penguin Classics, and Arkana—and how to order them, write to us at the appropriate address below. Please note that for copyright reasons the selection of books varies from country to country.

In the United States: Please write to *Consumer Sales, Penguin USA, P.O. Box 999, Dept. 17109, Bergenfield, New Jersey 07621-0120.* Visa and MasterCard holders call 1-800-253-6476 to order all Penguin titles.

In Canada: Please write to *Penguin Books Canada Ltd, 10 Alcorn Avenue, Suite 300, Toronto, Ontario M4V 3B2.*

In the United Kingdom: Please write to *Dept. JC, Penguin Books Ltd, FREEPOST, West Drayton, Middlesex UB7 OBR.*